JASON'S NEW DUGOUT CANOE

By Joe Barber-Starkey
Illustrated by Paul Montpellier

Harbour Publishing
P.O. Box 219, Madeira Park, BC Canada V0N 2H0

We acknowledge the financial support of the Government of Canada through the Book Publishing Industry Development Program for our publishing activities. We further acknowledge the support of the Canada Council for the Arts and the Province of British Columbia through the British Columbia Arts Council for our publishing program.

Book design by Martin Nichols, Lionheart Graphics
Endsheet illustration Roger Handling

Canadian Cataloguing in Publication Data

Barber-Starkey, Joe, 1918-
Jason's new dugout canoe

ISBN 1-55017-229-8

THE CANADA COUNCIL | LE CONSEIL DES ARTS
FOR THE ARTS | DU CANADA
SINCE 1957 | DEPUIS 1957

1. Nootka Indians--Juvenile fiction. 2. Canoes and canoeing--Juvenile fiction. I. Montpellier, Paul, 1949- II. Title.
PS8553.A743J37 2000   jC813'.54   C00-910764-9
PZ7.B2333Ja 2000

Printed in Hong Kong by Colorcraft Ltd

JASON was wakened in the night by the sounds of a winter storm. The wind was making a spooky howling noise, and sometimes there were sudden gusts which made the little house shake. The driving rain was rattling against his window and pushing under the roof shingles until it leaked through and made puddles on the floor. He tried to go back to sleep with his head under the blanket to keep out the noise, but he could still hear the storm and the crashing of waves on the beach.

Then suddenly, everything was still except for the sound of the surf and the rumble of big logs being rolled up the beach by the waves. Then even that sound died away. Jason got up, pulled on his jacket and boots and quietly went out of the house. The moon's light reflected on the white foam of the breakers as they rolled up the beach, rattling the stones as they slid down again. The wind started to blow again, but it was from a different direction and it was very cold, so Jason went back to his bed.

In the morning the storm had passed, but there were still big waves. When Jason looked out the window, he couldn't see his canoe, which had been pulled up on some logs on the beach. He ran out of the house with an awful feeling in his stomach that his most precious possession might have been washed away in the storm. He ran up and down the beach and behind the piles of logs, asking everyone he met whether they had seen his canoe, but there was no sign of it.

He loved his canoe because of the freedom that it had given him to go fishing, to go exploring and to visit with his animal friends. He felt very sad and empty as he slowly walked home to tell his mother and grandfather. For several days he kept looking, hoping that it might have been washed up on the shore somewhere. But a week later one of the fishermen found some pieces of the canoe a long way from where Jason had left it. Now he knew that it had been smashed to pieces by the storm.

Jason's sadness turned to joy several weeks later. His father and grandfather told him that they had asked his Uncle Silas, who was the canoe-maker for their village, to make Jason a new canoe. And they wanted Silas to teach him the skills which had been passed down to him from their ancestors for hundreds of years.

The task of being the canoe-maker was one of the most important and respected in the culture of the First Nations of the Northwest coast. This was because the dense forests, rocky shores and long inlets made travel by land nearly impossible, so the sea became their highway between villages and to otherwise inaccessible lands. Their canoes were made from the plentiful cedar trees.

They made many types and sizes of canoe to suit special uses, from the giant ocean-going war canoes and those which carried freight and many passengers to the one-person craft used for fishing. There were also special racing canoes of all sizes. Some of the bands had a tradition of hunting whales with a team of trained athletes paddling a specially made canoe.

Most families had their own canoes, and when they visited relatives, travelled between summer and winter villages, or attended special feasts and ceremonies at a central meeting place, they packed food, water, clothing, tools, and fishing gear into the traditional one-piece cedar boxes and loaded them into their canoes just as if they were today's family vans or station wagons!

When it was time to find a tree for Jason's new canoe, Jason, his father and Uncle Silas followed the trail up the river valley to the middle of a forest of red cedar trees. He could see the stumps of big trees that had been cut down to make canoes. Some trees that were still alive had·scars where planks had been split off or long pieces of bark had been pulled away to make baskets and mats.

The tree Uncle Silas picked out for Jason's canoe had no branches near the bottom because branches make knots. It was also big enough that they could take off part of the trunk without killing the tree. Starting with a half-round log would save the canoe-makers a lot of work. But before cutting the canoe block from the tree, Silas made a small square hole deep into the trunk, using a hammer and chisel, to make sure the tree was not hollow or rotten. He found that the wood was sound and solid. Then they paused while Silas said a prayer to show respect for the tree as a living creature and asked it for permission to use its wood.

To remove the canoe block from the tree two deep cuts were made. The distance between them was a bit more than the length of the canoe. To reach the top cut they used a small dead tree as a ladder. Big wedges were then hammered in from both sides until the block of wood split off. Uncle Silas told them that the block was too green to be used now and would have to be left to season till the spring. And until a lot of wood had been cut away, it was too heavy for them to carry back to the village, so they would have to leave it in the forest. Jason was very disappointed to hear that he would have to wait so long. It sounded as if he would not be able to go canoeing again until next fall.

During the long winter months Jason spent a lot of time in Uncle Silas' workshop. There he learned about the tools they would be using to make the dugout. He practiced using the sharp cutting tools—axes, adzes, chisels and knives—and Uncle Silas also showed him how to sharpen them. Jason was very nervous when he first used the adze. Swinging a sharp blade so close to his toes took some getting used to, but as he practiced shaping the wood, he soon gained confidence.

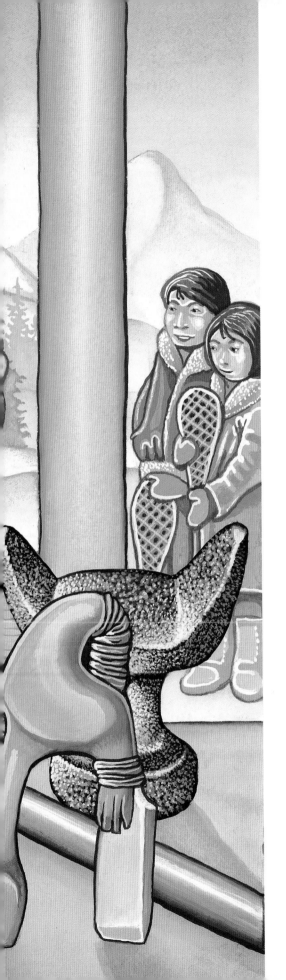

Silas also had a collection of tools with cutting edges made of stone, bone and shells which had been used many years ago before iron and steel had been brought to the coast. There were hammer-stones, too, specially shaped to fit the hand of the woodworker. Jason could now understand why in the olden days it had sometimes taken a year to make a canoe with tools like these.

When Captain Cook visited Nootka in 1778, he discovered that metal was the trade good most in demand by the local people. They had found knives and tools in the many shipwrecks that washed up on the stormy and rocky coast. Although they did not know the skills of a blacksmith, they found that long pieces of flat metal from the wrecks could be made into sharp blades by long hours of rubbing them on wet sandstone.

At last the warm days of Spring came, and Jason was very excited as they carried their tools up the trail to the cedar grove. When they got to the canoe log, Uncle Silas stripped off the bark and used a sharp knife to mark out the shape he wanted for the outside of the canoe. It was very important to have the measurements exactly equal from the centreline of the keel. This was to ensure that it would float level in the water and go in a straight line when it was paddled.

The outside of the canoe was shaped first, using axes and adzes, and then they rolled the block over to chop most of the wood out of the inside. This is why it is called a 'dugout.' Silas said that in the old days the inside was sometimes burned out with a carefully controlled fire. They worked for many weeks together, watched only by a pair of ravens perched on a branch above them. Silas said that was a sign that there was something very special about Jason's canoe.

With so much wood removed, the canoe was much lighter, so they asked three of Jason's friends to help them carry it on poles back to the village.

Jason felt very proud when it arrived there, and all his other friends clapped their hands and called out to him.

The next important job was to finish shaping the inside to be exactly the right thickness. The bottom had to be the strongest, thickest part and the top of the sides was to be only half as thick. To measure this, Silas drilled rows of holes from the outside and then made some round pegs that would fit the holes. Each peg was the exact length of the thickness which he wanted at that place. The ends of the pegs were blackened in a fire before being hammered into the right hole. When the carver was shaping the inside of the canoe, he would stop cutting when he saw the black marks.

It took many days to carefully finish the inside of the canoe, with Uncle Silas doing most of the work, but he often stopped to give Jason a chance to use the special curved chisels and knives.

Now came the most difficult task—spreading the sides of the canoe so that it would have a flat bottom and not tip easily. Also the sides would have to slope outwards to stop waves washing over the edge. If the spreading didn't go right the wood could split and ruin the canoe. Uncle Silas said that in the old times the canoe-maker would have to perform many rituals before he started this task and would not allow anyone else to watch the spreading process.

Silas built a fire and piled many stones around it to make them hot. Jason filled the canoe half full of water, and Silas picked up the hot stones with wooden tongs and dropped them in. When the water boiled, he covered the canoe with cedar mats so that the steam would soften the wood.

After a while Silas said the wood was soft enough to be shaped, so he cut some crosspieces a little longer than the width between the sides. He hammered these gently into place until the canoe sides spread. He continued this with other pieces, each a little bit longer, until he had the shape he wanted. Jason had a real scare when he heard a loud bang. He thought the canoe must have split, but it was only one of the stones that had exploded in the fire when it got too hot!

Stronger permanent crosspieces were installed to be used as seats. The bow and stern pieces were carved to shape and joined to the ends of the canoe with stitching, using the strong roots from a spruce tree.

All the splinters were then scorched off the canoe's sides and bottom with a piece of burning wood. The outside was rubbed smooth with sandstone and a piece of rough dogfish skin to make the canoe ready for painting.

At last the canoe was finished and it was time to celebrate! The people of the village gathered around a big fire on the beach and shared a feast of salmon cooked in their traditional way. Pieces of fish were spread flat, using cedar skewers woven crossways on upright sticks and placed close to the fire. Later on as it got dark, the people danced and told stories. Grandfather sang a song which had first been sung hundreds of years ago, about a great hunter of whales and his canoe.

Then Jason's canoe was carried down to the water, and Uncle Silas gave Jason a paddle he had carved from maple wood. To the sound of clapping and cheering Jason paddled out into the bay, proud of having learned to build his own canoe. He stopped and listened to the quiet lapping of the night waves on the shore. As he lay back and looked at the sparkle of the starry night, he wondered what to call his canoe. He decided that a good name would be 'Sea Otter,' after his animal friends.

After that, Jason had many happy days with his new canoe. Sometimes he went fishing. Sometimes he went exploring and visiting animals and birds on the sandy beaches and in the rocky coves around the coast near his village. He also visited some of the islands nearby, and on one of these he found where the two ravens had built their nest. But the times that he enjoyed most were when he could visit his animal friends, the sea otters.

After the long months of waiting he realized how important the canoe was in his life, and he thought that it would be nice if other children could learn about the freedom it could give them. Perhaps when he grew up, he could become a canoe-maker like Uncle Silas and make canoes for other children.